One World

THE HISTORY AND GOVERNMENT OF East and Southeast Asia

JILL KEPPELER

PowerKiDS press.

Published in 2021 by The Rosen Publishing Group, Inc.
29 East 21st Street, New York, NY 10010

First Edition

Editor: Caitie McAneney
Book Design: Seth Hughes

Photo Credits: Cover (top) zhao jiankang/Shutterstock.com; cover (bottom) Vietnam Stock Images/Shutterstock.com; p. 5 Jose Fuste Raga/Corbis Documentary/Getty Images; p. 8 (top) Print Collector/Hulton Archive/Getty Images; p. 8 (bottom) Jason_YU/iStock/Getty Images; p. 9 Luis Davilla/Stone/Getty Images; p. 10 fannrei/iStock Editorial/Getty Images; p. 12 (both) Werner Forman/Universal Images Group/Getty Images; p. 13 VW Pics/Universal Images Group/Getty Images; p. 15 Gilles BASSIGNAC/Gamma-Rapho/Getty Images; p. 16 (top) Luis Castaneda Inc./The Image Bank/Getty Images; pp. 16 (bottom), 31 Universal History Archive/Universal Images Group/Getty Images; p. 17 mTaira/Shutterstock.com; pp. 19, 28 Eric Lafforgue/Art in All of Us/Corbis News/Getty Images; p. 21 xia yuan/Moment/Getty Images; p. 22 Heritage Images/Hulton Fine Art Collection/Getty Images; p. 23 https://upload.wikimedia.org/wikipedia/commons/2/23/Lang_Ngô_Quy.n.jpg; p. 25 Wolfgang Kaehler/LightRocket/Getty Images; p. 26 (top) Carl Court/Getty Images News/Getty Images; p. 26 (bottom) heckepics/iStock/Getty Images; p. 27 RJ Sangosti/Denver Post/Getty Images; p. 29 Heritage Images/Hulton Archive/Getty Images; p. 30 PHAS/Universal Images Group/Getty Images; p. 32 Jim Dyson/Getty Images News/Getty Images; p. 35 Print Collector/Hulton Archive/Getty Images; p. 37 (top) Bernard Hoffman/The LIFE Picture Collection/Getty Images; p. 37 (bottom) Hulton Archive/Archive Photos/Getty Images; p. 38 Hulton Archive/Getty Images; p. 39 (top) Keystone/Hulton Archive/Getty Images; p. 39 (bottom) Terry Fincher/Hulton Archive/Getty Images; p. 40 Lintao Zhang/Getty Images News/Getty Images; p. 41 STR/AFP/Getty Images; p. 42 Pool/Getty Images News/Getty Images; p. 43 SAUL LOEB/AFP/Getty Images; p. 45 Bettmann/Getty Images.

Cataloging-in-Publication Data
Names: Keppeler, Jill.
Title: The history and government of East and Southeast Asia / Jill Keppeler.
Description: New York : PowerKids Press, 2021. | Series: One world | Includes glossary and index.
Identifiers: ISBN 9781725321441 (pbk.) | ISBN 9781725321465 (library bound) | ISBN 9781725322134 (6 pack) | ISBN 9781725322035 (ebook)
Subjects: LCSH: East Asia–Juvenile literature. | East Asia–History–Juvenile literature. | East Asia–Politics and government–Juvenile literature. | Southeast Asia–Juvenile literature. | Southeast Asia–History–Juvenile literature. | Southeast Asia–Politics and government–Juvenile literature.
Classification: LCC DS504.5 K46 2021 | DDC 950–dc23

Manufactured in the United States of America

CPSIA Compliance Information: Batch #CSPK20: For Further Information contact Rosen Publishing, New York, New York at 1-800-237-9932

CONTENTS

Introduction

EAST AND SOUTHEAST ASIA

Asia is the world's largest continent, full of diverse peoples and governments. East and Southeast Asia include about 20 countries today, born out of some of the world's oldest civilizations. From China—the world's third-largest country with the world's largest population—to the city-state of Singapore, the countries of east and Southeast Asia have a rich history and varied forms of government.

Ancient China, one of the first civilizations to arise anywhere in the world, had a profound effect on the countries that grew and developed

diverse: Different or varied.

city-state: A political division made up of a city and surrounding area.

The city of Beijing is the capital of the People's Republic of China. It's been an important part of China's history for more than 800 years.

around it. The countries of east Asia, including China, Japan, North Korea, South Korea, Taiwan, Mongolia, Hong Kong, and Macau, contain about 22 percent of the world's population and some of the world's biggest cities, such as Tokyo and Beijing.

The 11 countries of Southeast Asia—Myanmar (also called Burma), Thailand, Laos, Cambodia, Vietnam, Malaysia, Singapore, Indonesia, the Philippines, Brunei, and Timor-Leste (also called East Timor)—include both mainland and island nations. The region's geography has made it a meeting place for trade throughout the centuries.

The diversity of these nations extends to their governments as well. Some have a limited government with a constitution and some form of **democracy**, while others have an unlimited government with a dictatorship.

limited government: A government led by the citizens in which everyone, including all authority figures, must obey the laws.

unlimited government: A government in which control is placed solely with the ruler and their appointees, and there are no limits imposed on their authority.

dictatorship: A government in which the leader has unlimited power and severely limits the rights of the citizens.

Chapter One

ANCIENT ASIA

Fossils show that **hominins**, including the now-extinct *Homo erectus* and the modern human species *Homo sapiens*, have lived in Asia for at least 1 million years. In fact, they may have lived there much longer. Prehistoric human populations in the region likely centered on north China and the plateaus of Mongolia, **migrating** from there to other locations in the region. Scientists found the first-known set of fossils for *Homo erectus*, which they named Java man, on the island of Java, Indonesia, in the 1890s. Other scientists found a later set of fossils, called Peking man, near Beijing, China. Both date back hundreds of thousands of years.

hominin: Any of a group of two-footed primate mammals, including humans and their extinct ancestors, such as Neanderthals.

migrate: To move from one region to another.

This photo shows the jawbone and teeth of Java man, a set of Homo erectus *fossils found in Indonesia.*

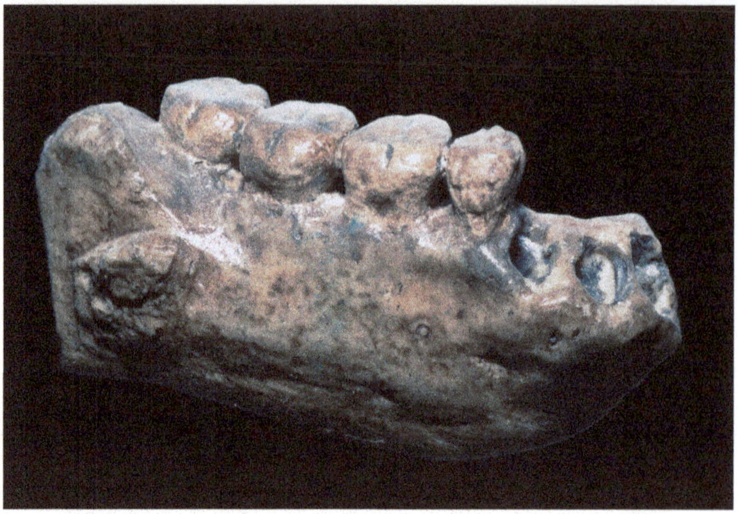

ANCIENT INDONESIA

Indonesia, an **archipelago** off mainland Southeast Asia, includes more than 17,500 small islands. While early hominins such as *Homo erectus* did live on the islands, DNA testing suggests that modern humans (*Homo sapiens*) first came to Indonesia more than 50,000 years ago. By 300 BC, there were Hindu kingdoms on the islands of Java and Sumatra. Soon after, there were likely Buddhist kingdoms as well. Monsoon winds helped early sailors travel between islands, increasing communication and trade with the rest of the region and even beyond.

The Yellow River, or Huang He, is the second-longest river in China. The first ancient civilizations in the region centered around this river.

monsoon: Seasonal winds that affect climate in the southern areas of Asia, resulting in wet spring and summer months and dry winter months.

History in FOCUS

Scholars believe the first humans to eat cooked food lived in southern China. They've found pots that may have been used for cooking at sites in Jiangxi and Guangxi, China.

The Yellow River valley in what's now China is sometimes called the cradle of Chinese civilization. In this valley and in areas of Southeast Asia, farming communities began growing rice and millet, a kind of grain, by 3500 BC. Over time, a number of **Neolithic**-period settlements grew in the region, including the Hongshan and Yangshao cultures of China, the cultures of the Korean peninsula, and the Jomon culture of Japan.

Rice has been a staple in the diets of the peoples of east and Southeast Asia for thousands of years. Rice fields like this one are found throughout the region.

The Jomon culture is generally accepted as the earliest major culture of the area now called Japan. It began sometime between 10,500 BC and 4500 BC. Scholars disagree about when the Jomon civilization originated, though most agree that it ended around 300 BC. Archaeologists have found the remains of small Jomon communities throughout the islands, including distinctive pottery and stone and bone tools. The Yayoi culture followed, starting on the island of Kyushu and spreading northeast. It lasted about 550 years. Today, many members of the Ainu, an **indigenous** people of Japan, claim connection to the Jomon culture.

This is a recreated house from the Jomon period in Aomori ***Prefecture****, Japan.*

indigenous: Describing groups that are native to a particular region.

The first **dynasty** of China, the Xia dynasty, may have started between 2100 and 2070 BC, lasting until around 1600 BC. Some legends and archaeological sites point to this dynasty beginning under the emperor Yu. Also called Yu the Great, he is said to have established systems of flood control in the region.

LEGENDS OF THE YU DYNASTY

In Chinese mythology, Yu (or Da Yu) is also called the Tamer of the Flood. According to legends, he spent 13 years draining the waters of a huge flood from China with the help of a yellow dragon and a black turtle. Then he made his family the **hereditary** rulers of the area, making them the first dynasty. Stories say the dynasty had 17 rulers and that the last one, a man named Jie, married an evil woman and became a dictator. This caused a rebellion and led to the rise of the Shang dynasty. People still disagree on whether the Xia dynasty existed or was only a legend.

The Bronze Age was underway in the region by 1600 BC, with people using bronze metal tools and weapons. By this time, China had its first historically verified, or proven, dynasty—and its first written records. The records said that a tribal chief named Cheng Tang defeated the Xia dynasty and started the Shang dynasty about that time.

The engraved characters on this bone, which dates from the Shang dynasty in China, are some of the earliest known examples of Chinese writing.

This decorative building in Indonesia houses a bronze Dong-Son drum, created around 300 BC.

History in FOCUS

The Dong-Son culture of northern Vietnam started sometime between 1000 and 600 BC. It's known for the giant bronze drums its people created, which have been found throughout Southeast Asia.

Chapter Two

EMPERORS AND DYNASTIES

There were many advances during the Shang dynasty in China, including the art of bronze casting, a calendar system, and the development of the Chinese writing system, which is still important to the culture today. The Shang dynasty established Anyang as the capital around 1400 BC.

This chariot, found in Henan Province, China, is from the Shang dynasty. Chariots were ancient vehicles, pulled by animals such as horses.

The Shang dynasty fell around 1046 BC, leading into the Zhou dynasty. The Zhou ruled for about the next 800 years—the single longest period of Chinese history. The Zhou dynasty created the idea of the mandate of heaven. This was the belief that the true leader of China had the blessing of the gods and that there could only be one real leader at any given time. It was a form of unlimited government.

Early in the Zhou dynasty, the rulers controlled a network of feudal states, though this system broke down later. By 475 BC, China entered a period of wars and unrest, called the Warring States period. The last Zhou ruler died in 256 BC, and the Qin dynasty took over in 221 BC.

History in FOCUS

During the Warring States period in China, seven small kingdoms fought among themselves, with the Qin finally winning. Many of China's long-term governmental structures started during this time.

feudal: Relating to feudalism, a system in which people worked and fought for nobles who gave them protection and the use of land in return.

THE QIN DYNASTY

The Qin dynasty marked the beginning of imperial China, a time when the region was ruled by emperors. This imperial period stretched thousands of years, until AD 1912. The first emperor, Qin Shi Huang, had unlimited power, although he did have many aides. He did away with the remains of the feudal system and created the system of prefectures and counties. He called for the creation of many highways to move troops and administrators. He also started the construction of the Great Wall of China. The Qin dynasty itself, however, didn't last very long. By 206 BC, the Han dynasty took over.

The famous terra-cotta soldiers of China, first discovered in 1974, were part of the burial site of the first emperor, Qin Shi Huang. There are more than 8,000 clay soldiers in all, as well as chariots, horses, and weapons.

The first parts of the Great Wall of China date from the time of Chinese emperor Qin Shi Huang, around 220 BC. Running thousands of miles long, the Great Wall can be seen from space.

This drawing shows a Han dynasty general attacking **nomadic** *invaders called the Huns in 99 BC.*

Throughout the region of east and Southeast Asia, the imperial period was a time of growing populations, as well as of emperors and dynasties. The legendary Jimmu became the first emperor of Japan around 660 BC, and according to legend, he was followed by about 13 other emperors.

nomadic: Having to do with people who move from place to place.

History in FOCUS

Jimmu, the legendary first emperor of Japan, was said to be a descendant of the sun goddess Amaterasu. The belief in the divinity, or godliness, of the emperor continued for thousands of years.

This shrine is part of the Kashima Jingu Shrine in eastern Japan. It was allegedly built by the first emperor of Japan, Jimmu, in the sixth century BC.

THE XIONGNU

In the region of Mongolia, a people called the Xiongnu (likely the ancestors of the Mongols) created a great tribal empire during the time of the Qin and Han dynasties in China. Their attempted invasions of China led to the building of the Great Wall of China. The many tribes of the Xiongnu came together around 300 BC under a ruler called the *chanyu*. As their raids continued, in time, the Han emperor started aggressively sending out expeditions against them. This led to greater Chinese exploration and conquest of the region. When the Xiongnu eventually broke up, some of them were absorbed into China.

Today's Vietnam also has a history based heavily on legend. Stories say that the 18 kings of the Hung dynasty ruled a region called Van Lang, which included part of southern China. Around 258 BC, a warlord named Thuc Phan took over Van Lang, creating the kingdom of Au Lac. Then, around 207 BC, a former Chinese general took over this kingdom, creating another. This one was called Nam Viet. One of the Han emperors of China later conquered it.

The first Korean kingdom was known as Old Chosôn (or Gojoseon). It was started in the northern part of the area and spread by conquering and absorbing smaller nearby provinces. Legend says it was founded around 2333 BC by Tan'gun. He was said to be the son of a god and a bear-turned-woman. Old Chosôn fell sometime in the first century BC.

This is the mausoleum, or tomb, of Tan'gun, the first king of the Korean people.

Chapter Three

CONNECTING TO THE WIDER WORLD

The challenging geography of east and Southeast Asia sometimes isolated it, or kept it apart, from other areas. From the vast deserts and high mountains of China to the wide areas of ocean between Southeast Asian islands, many cultures developed largely without outside influences.

History in FOCUS

Confucius (551 BC–479 BC) was perhaps the most famous Chinese thinker to ever live. His political and philosophical teachings shaped life in east Asia and continue to influence the area today.

However, around 130 BC, the Han dynasty established famous trade routes that were collectively called the Silk Road, connecting China and surrounding regions with the West. The 4,000-mile (6,437.4 km) route linked the region with Southwest Asian and European countries, including ancient Rome. The Silk Road led to the exchange of ideas as well as goods such as silk and precious metals.

The Stone Fort in Tashkurgan, China, shown here, dates back to sixth century AD. It sits at an important spot on the Silk Road trade route.

This piece of artwork from the medieval Catalan Atlas shows a caravan, or group of travelers, on the Silk Road.

The Han dynasty faded by the end of the second century AD, and smaller dynasties and kingdoms fought for power. By AD 581, the Sui dynasty **unified** China again. Sui emperors started reaching out to their neighbors in east and Southeast Asia—for better or worse.

China established a relationship with Japan but started military campaigns in Korea. The campaigns didn't go well for the Sui dynasty and led, in part, to its fall and the rise of the Tang dynasty in AD 618. The Tang dynasty marked a golden age in ancient China, where technology, art, and poetry flourished. The Tang dynasty ended around AD 907, followed soon after by the Song dynasty.

unify: To bring separate parts together into one unit.

CIVIL SERVICE AND BUREAUCRACY

One notable part of imperial China's government was the civil service system. Under the Qin dynasty, the empire developed its own centralized bureaucracy and needed people to staff it. The next few dynasties dealt with this in different ways and eventually developed a system of strict schooling and testing to determine who would enter the civil service. Starting under the Tang dynasty, about AD 650, students would take part in the difficult *jinshi* exams, which tested would-be bureaucrats largely on the writings of Chinese philosophers like Confucius. Those who did well could become high officials in the government. This system lasted in China until AD 1905.

History in FOCUS

Today's Vietnam region was under Chinese rule for more than a thousand years. However, Ngo Quyen, a Vietnamese commander, defeated the Chinese in AD 939, starting a period of independence.

The tomb of Vietnamese commander-turned-ruler Ngo Quyen (AD 897–944) stands in Hanoi, Vietnam.

bureaucracy: An administrative, policy-making group.

Within a period lasting from around 57 BC to AD 668, Korea consisted of three rival kingdoms: Koguryô, Paekche, and Silla. All three kingdoms had central power, centralized military systems, and aristocracies. Silla had a council of nobles that helped make important decisions. By AD 668, Silla had taken over the other two kingdoms with the help of China. Then, the kingdom drove out the Chinese and controlled the Korean Peninsula, developing into an absolute monarchy for a time.

SRIVIJAYA AND MAJAPAHIT

By about the seventh century AD, the powerful Buddhist kingdom of Srivijaya arose on the Indonesian island of Sumatra. Its power was based on overseas trade, both with other islands and with China and India. Srivijaya controlled much of Indonesia until about AD 1290, when the Hindu empire of Majapahit, which originated on the island of Java, took over. Over more than 200 years, this empire would unite most of what are today Indonesia and Malaysia. Traders from Islamic countries also began spreading their faith in the region through the islands' ports, leading to a mix of religions in the area.

monarchy: A government ruled by one person with absolute power.

This Buddhist temple from the eighth century AD stands on the island of Java, Indonesia. Buddhism originated in India around the sixth century BC and spread through trade routes.

During the early centuries AD, Japan had many small kingdoms, but these gradually became increasingly unified in the Yamato state (or kingdom) in the fourth and fifth centuries. The Japanese had **diplomatic** relationships with China and the kingdoms of Korea, connecting to and sharing with the peoples of the region. Japan borrowed many cultural elements from these places, including Buddhism from Korea and writing systems from China. This started the time of so-called classical Japan around AD 500, which ended in the Heian period in AD 1185.

In this photograph from 2018, people dressed as nobles of Japan's Heian period take part in the Aoi Festival in Kyoto, Japan.

History in FOCUS

China's Song dynasty ended during the 1200s. Starting in 1211, Mongol tribes (united and led by Genghis Khan) began conquering much of the region. Genghis Khan's grandson, Kublai Khan, officially took over and started the Mongol dynasty—also called the Yuan dynasty—in 1279.

This enormous statue of Mongolian conqueror Genghis Khan (AD 1162–1227) stands today in Mongolia. One of the most famous warrior-rulers in history, Khan created a unified Mongolia and extended his reach across Asia.

Chapter Four

RISE OF THE COLONIAL ERA

Not long after the classical period ended in Japan around 1185, the warrior **caste**, or samurai, took power and a new era began. In 1192, this new government was officially labeled a shogunate, which was a government run by a **shogun**. The emperor was still a legal authority, but the shogun appointed his own military governors and held most of the power. This lasted until the Meiji Restoration of the late 19th century returned power to the imperial dynasty.

This set of samurai armor from Japan dates from the shogunate, from about the 17th to the 18th centuries.

shogun: One of a line of military governors ruling Japan until the revolution of 1867–68.

In Korea, a new Chosôn dynasty, also called the Yi dynasty, took power and lasted from 1392 to 1910. This wasn't without challenges. In the late 1500s, the region helped hold off Japanese attempts to invade China, but it suffered many losses in the process.

This royal villa in what is now North Korea was once the home of Yi Song-Gye, who founded the Chosôn dynasty in 1392.

By the 14th century, after the Ming dynasty arose, things gradually became more **urbanized** in China. Cities, including Nanjing and Beijing, grew, as did forms of industry. At times, the dynasty restricted trade with other countries, but this eventually changed in the 16th century.

The Chinese Ming dynasty was known for its pottery, or ceramics, such as works like this blue and white vase. Because the Chinese started this craft, ceramics are sometimes called "china," and they are considered fine goods.

European countries such as Portugal, Spain, and the Netherlands flocked to the area for trade. Neighboring east Asian countries did too, sharing goods and ideas. Products from some European-controlled countries in the "New World," such as Peru and Mexico, also found their way to the area.

The Silk Road had connected China and other Asian countries to Europe by land. However, European countries started searching for better trade routes to Asia, leading to the Age of Exploration. During this time, explorers from various European powers sailed the world, taking control of trade in many areas. This, in turn, led to the rise of colonization.

THE PHILIPPINES

The Philippines is an island country consisting of an archipelago of more than 7,500 islands off the coast of Vietnam. The Philippine islands are part of the Ring of Fire. The name comes from King Philip II, who ruled Spain when the Spanish colonized the islands in the 1500s. Its capital is Manila, located on Luzon, its largest island. The Spanish held it for 333 years. After the Spanish-American War in 1898, the United States took over, although the Philippine people wanted independence. Nearly 50 years later, in 1946, they finally became independent.

This picture shows Miguel López de Legaspi, the Spanish explorer who established control over the Philippines in the 1500s.

colonization: The act of making or establishing a settlement in a new territory that maintains ties to a distant parent state.

Ring of Fire: An area where large numbers of earthquakes and volcanic eruptions occur in the basin of the Pacific Ocean.

Portugal found sea access to Asia first, around 1500, and claimed small coastal areas in the region. Spain took over the Philippines starting in 1565. By 1605, the Dutch East India Company had established control over a good part of Indonesia and the valuable spice trade there.

This picture shows the city of Bantam in Java, Indonesia, in 1750. This Southeast Asian city was an important port for the spice trade with Europe.

As time went on, Great Britain established colonies in Southeast Asia too, in areas that are now known as Myanmar, Singapore, Malaysia, parts of Indonesia, and Hong Kong. France took Vietnam, Laos, and Cambodia.

These statues stand outside the Grand Palace in Bangkok, Thailand. The palace has been the home of the leaders of Thailand (formerly Siam) since the 1700s.

History in FOCUS

The country of Siam permanently changed its name to Thailand in 1949. It is the only country in Southeast Asia that was never colonized by Europeans. It was an absolute monarchy until 1932. Today, it is a **constitutional monarchy**.

constitutional monarchy: A system of government in which a country is ruled by a monarch whose power is limited by a constitution.

THE OPIUM WARS

The increased presence of Europeans in Asia had many effects. In 1839, China tried to stop the trade of opium by foreign visitors, mostly the British. Opium is a harmful drug people become addicted to, or hooked on. The Qing dynasty tried to ban opium, which was causing an addiction crisis. So, the British shut down Chinese ports and captured Nanjing. A treaty forced China to give Great Britain the island of Hong Kong and various privileges. The second Opium War started in 1856, when Britain and France demanded China legalize opium. In the end, China had to give the countries even more power in the region.

History in FOCUS

The island of Taiwan was formerly a Dutch colony, a Chinese province, and part of the Japanese empire. Today, there is debate over whether it's an independent country or part of China.

Chapter Five

MODERN WARS

The 20th century was a time of upheaval for east and Southeast Asia, including two world wars, fading colonization, foreign conflicts, changes in philosophy and government, increasing industrialization, and globalization.

In 1912, China became the Republic of China, ending the age of dynasties. Conflict between China and Japan was heating up. In 1914, World War I exploded, pitting the Central Powers—Austria-Hungary, Bulgaria, Germany, and the Ottoman Empire—against the Allies, which included Britain, France, Italy, Russia, and eventually the United States. Japan joined the Allies later in 1914, and China joined in 1917.

globalization: The development of an increasingly connected global economy marked by free trade and free flow of capital.

World War I ended in 1918 with an Allied victory. However, relations between China and Japan became even worse with the war-ending Treaty of Versailles, which gave Japan some of Germany's possessions in Shandong, China. The Chinese government's response to protests over this led to the rise of **communism**. In 1921, the Communist Party of China formed.

This picture shows British Prime Minister David Lloyd George signing the Treaty of Versailles in 1919 France. The treaty ended World War I but caused much fallout in east Asia.

communism: A way of organizing society where there is no privately owned property.

Japan began a series of military conquests to expand. In 1931, Japan invaded the region of Manchuria in China, increasing its territory in the region over the next few years. Around the same time, conflicts between Chinese communists and nationalists turned into a civil war. The fighting lasted from 1927 to late 1936. Then, in early 1937, the second Sino-Japanese War between Japan and China exploded. Japan took the cities of Shanghai and Nanjing in 1937.

World War II started in 1939, in part growing out of the Japanese invasion of China. Japan joined the Axis powers (Germany and Italy), while China joined the Allied Powers (Great Britain, the Soviet Union, and the United States). The conflict affected Southeast Asia, including the Philippines, Burma, and Singapore, leaving devastation behind. In early August 1945, the United States dropped two atomic bombs on the Japanese cities of Hiroshima and Nagasaki, killing more than 140,000 people. Japan surrendered, and World War II finally came to an end.

nationalist: Supporting national independence.

A man stands in the rubble left behind by the U.S. bombing of Hiroshima, Japan, in late 1945.

Aboard the USS Missouri in Tokyo Bay, General Yoshijiro Umezu of Japan signs a document of surrender on September 2, 1945. U.S. General George MacArthur (center) watches.

History in FOCUS

After World War II, the U.S. government occupied Japan, creating sweeping social, economic, political, and military reforms. Japan regained independence in 1952.

The communist conflict in China continued, however. The civil war started up again in 1945. In 1949, the civil war in China between nationalists and communists ended violently. The People's Republic of China, under Communist Party chairman Mao Zedong, took power.

In this 1938 photograph, Chinese Communist Party leader Mao Zedong calls for greater efforts against the Japanese.

History in FOCUS

After World War II, Taiwan became part of China, which led to rebellion and conflict. Today, Taiwan is called the Republic of China (which is separate from the People's Republic of China on the mainland).

The Cold War (1945–1991) began, pitting the democracies of the western world against the communism of the Soviet Union. The Korean War and the Vietnam War began as a response to this conflict of ideologies.

THE KOREAN WAR (1950–1953)

When the Japanese empire collapsed after World War II, the Soviet Union and the United States divided Korea, which had been **annexed** by Japan in 1910. The northern part of Korea became the Democratic People's Republic of Korea, backed by the communist Soviet Union. The southern part of Korea became the Republic of Korea, backed by the democratic United States and the United Nations. In June 1950, North Korea invaded South Korea. The United States feared a communist campaign might take over the world and sent troops to the conflict. China sent troops to aid North Korea. Fighting finally ended in 1953, but the Koreas remain divided today.

A woman and her grandchild stand by the ruins of their home in Pyongyang, the capital of North Korea, after a 1950 air raid by U.S. planes during the Korean War.

History in FOCUS

The United States got involved in the Korean War and Vietnam War because of the "domino theory." The idea was that if one Southeast Asian country fell to communism, others would follow.

THE VIETNAM WAR (1955–1975)

In 1954, France left Vietnam after many years of controlling it as a colony. North Vietnam and its allies in the south, called the Viet Cong, wanted to unify the country under a communist government. However, south Vietnam held strong to democratic principles. The United States, an ally of south Vietnam, worried about the spread of communism. It poured hundreds of thousands of U.S. troops into the conflict. As the war expanded across the country, at least 2 million Vietnamese civilians died, in addition to soldiers on each side. The United States withdrew its troops by 1973, and South Vietnam fell two years later. In Vietnam, the war is known as "The American War."

American soldiers and Vietnamese refugees are shown in the town of Hue in Vietnam in 1968.

refugee: A migrant person who flees their homeland to escape disaster, persecution, or war.

Chapter Six

GOVERNMENTS TODAY

Today, China and Japan are both considered world powers. The People's Republic of China is still largely governed by the Chinese Communist Party (CCP). There are elections in China and a constitution (adopted in 1982), but the CCP dominates this government. The National People's Congress elects the State Council and president.

Chinese President Xi Jinping speaks in 2017 in Beijing. He leads the Communist Party of China, the dominant political party in the republic.

THE POWER OF TRADE AND INDUSTRY

In the 20th century, international trade (especially with the United States) led to increased industrialization in east and Southeast Asia. In Southeast Asia, much of the industrial development has taken place since the 1960s. The region supplies cheap labor for Western countries. China didn't have much of a part in the world economy until the late 1900s. This has changed immensely since then, and the country is now a major player in world trade. Japan built influential trade relationships with the West earlier than others in the region. Despite its position in World War II, Japan rebounded afterward to become the world's second-biggest economic power.

Japan is a constitutional monarchy. The emperor remains a ceremonial ruler and a symbol of the country, but there are three branches of government—executive (prime minister and cabinet), legislative (called the National Diet), and judicial. There are multiple political parties in Japan, and all Japanese citizens 18 years or older can vote in elections.

Japanese Emperer Naruhito and Empress Masako take part in a royal parade in Tokyo in November 2019. Naruhito took the throne as Japan's 126th emperor in May 2019.

U.S. President Barack Obama meets with Japan Prime Minister Shinzo Abe on March 25, 2018, in Tokyo, during Obama's trip there for an international conference.

Different government systems exist in the rest of the region. Thailand has a constitutional monarchy. The Philippines, Indonesia, South Korea, Laos, and Vietnam all have some form of republic. However, a country can be called a republic and still not give its people a fair voice in government. Vietnam, like China, effectively only has one dominant political party—the Communist Party. In Laos, the Lao People's Revolutionary Party is the only legally recognized political party. These are unitary systems.

North Korea has a **totalitarian** government. It's considered one of the world's most **repressive** states, and its leader has almost total political

republic: A form of government in which people elect representatives to legislate.

unitary system: A national government that performs all government functions.

power. The government restricts, or limits, any political opposition. North Korea also restricts civil rights and has taken part in harmful human rights violations.

North Korean leader Kim Jong-Un and U.S. president Donald Trump meet on June 12, 2018, in Singapore. Various U.S. presidents have tried to negotiate, or bargain, with North Korea, with few highs and many lows in diplomacy.

History in FOCUS

A mixed economy allows for both a free market and governmental intervention. China and the United States both have mixed economies. North Korea has a command economy, controlled completely by the government.

Other countries in east and Southeast Asia have struggled with human rights issues. China has shut down public protests that

human rights: Universal rights possessed by all people in the world because they are a human being.

mixed economy: An economy that allows for both public and private ownership of businesses.

command economy: An economy in which the government controls all production and distribution of goods and services.

oppose government actions. The government has arrested, tortured, and executed people of religious minorities and those who'd like to change the country's government. The Chinese government has held Uigher Muslims in prison camps, trying to "re-educate" them by force, and has **oppressed** the people of Tibet. The government has tight control over the news media and internet. Cambodia, Thailand, Vietnam, Indonesia, Myanmar, and other countries in the region have used violence against political activists, religious minorities, and other protesters.

CALLS FOR DEMOCRACY

Throughout the years, activists have called for greater freedom and rights in China. In the spring and summer of 1989, huge protests called the Tiananmen Square demonstrations took place. This led to the Tiananmen Square Massacre, in which the Chinese government violently put down unrest on June 3 and 4. Tanks and troops shot or crushed student protesters, with a death toll in the hundreds or thousands. The government arrested around 10,000 protesters, executing some of them. People in Hong Kong have also called for democracy over the years. Starting in June 2019, millions of people took to the streets in Hong Kong to protest a bill allowing **extradition** to China. While the bill was withdrawn, the protests and calls for change have continued.

This famous photograph from June 1989 shows a protester standing in front of a tank near China's Tiananmen Square.

History in FOCUS

China took over Hong Kong from British rule in 1997. Since then, there have been many calls for the human rights that were supposed to be guaranteed to Hong Kong's people.

Protesters gather on June 26, 2019, in Hong Kong, calling for the end of an extradition bill and for greater rights for Hong Kong residents.

East and Southeast Asia are regions with long and rich histories of flourishing dynasties and cultures, shifting boundaries, and bloody wars. As the nations of this region join the global community, calls for democracy ring loud. The region is likely to see more change as it moves into the future.

History in FOCUS

Wuhan is the capital city of the Hubei province in central China. In 2019, an outbreak of the deadly COVID-19 virus was first reported in Wuhan. As the virus spread, it put great stress on the Chinese government and other governments around the world.

GLOSSARY

annex: To take over an area and make it part of a larger territory.

archipelago: A group of islands.

caste: A division of society based on differences including rank or job.

democracy: A form of government in which people choose leaders by voting, directly or indirectly.

diplomatic: Having peaceful communication between nations.

dynasty: A family of rulers who rule over a country for a long time.

extradition: The act of sending someone who's been accused of a crime to another state or country for trial.

hereditary: Passed down from generation to generation.

Neolithic: Relating to the time during the Stone Age when people used stone tools and began to grow crops, raise animals, and live together in large groups but did not read or write.

oppress: To unjustly use power over another; to treat people in a cruel or unfair way.

prefecture: An area into which some countries are divided for local government.

repressive: Controlling or putting people down by force.

totalitarian: Relating to centralized control by an unlimited leader; also, relating to a government that controls all aspects of the lives of its citizens and national productivity, especially by force.

urbanized: Having undergone urbanization, or the process by which towns and cities are formed and become larger as more and more people begin living and working in central areas.

FOR MORE INFORMATION

BOOKS:

Adams, Simon. *The Kingfisher Atlas of World History*. New York, NY: Kingfisher, 2016.

Duggar, Kayla. *Timelines of Everything*. New York, NY: DK Publishing, 2018.

Manzanero, Paula. *The Who Was? History of the World*. New York, NY: Penguin Workshop, 2019.

WEBSITES:

Ancient China
www.dkfindout.com/us/history/ancient-china/
Learn more about one of the world's oldest civilizations on the DK Find Out! website.

10 Facts About World War II
www.natgeokids.com/au/discover/history/general-history/world-war-two/
World War II had a huge impact on east and Southeast Asia and the world. Learn more here through National Geographic.

Types of Government
mocomi.com/types-of-government/
This interactive website describes types of governments and how they work.

Publisher's note to educators and parents: Our editors have carefully reviewed these websites to ensure that they are suitable for students. Many websites change frequently, however, and we cannot guarantee that a site's future contents will continue to meet our high standards of quality and educational value. Be advised that students should be closely supervised whenever they access the internet.

INDEX